Royal Fun!

By Bill Scollon

Life in Enchancia is full of fun!
There are so many things to do.
The king and queen love to dance.

Sofia didn't know how to dance when she first came to live at the castle. But with practice, she's getting better all the time!

Sofia is the first princess to try out for Royal Prep's flying derby team! She's been practicing with her pint-sized flying horse, Minimus.

The spectators can't wait to see
Sofia and Minimus compete with
the princes. On your wings.
Get set. Go!

Sofia and Minimus are doing well in the race until they lose their balance and fall to the ground! But that doesn't stop Sofia.

She gets back on Minimus and they race to the finish line. Sofia and James win first and second places and qualify for the flying derby team!

Spending the day at the Village Faire is lots of fun! Amber, Sofia, and James enjoy the attractions, the music, and all the delicious food!

A stilt-walking jester entertains the crowds with all sorts of magic tricks, and showers the royal children with a rainbow of confetti!

Then acrobats come back to the castle to entertain Sofia and her family. They leap, bounce, and tumble around the Throne Room.

Everyone claps for the talented tumblers.

"Brilliant!" says James.

"Magnificent," calls King Roland.

"Way to go!" shouts Sofia.

There's nothing more fun than a slumber party! Sofia and Amber invite their friends to the castle for a royal sleepover.

They get makeovers and play fun party
games, and Cedric, the royal sorcerer,
even performs a magic puppet show.
The girls laugh and laugh!

At first, Amber and her princess friends don't think Sofia's pinecone curlers are proper for a royal slumber party.

But when they see how much fun they're missing, they join in and everyone has a great time together!

Use the play scenes and magnets to create your own royal fun!